PICK UP THE GUN, MY SON

The 1951 Western and Its Appalachian Pulp Author

David Arrate

My Kind of Story

Copyright © 2025 David Arrate

All rights reserved. No part of this publication may be reproduced, distributed, or transmitted in any form or by any means, including photocopying, recording, or other electronic or mechanical methods, without the prior written permission of the author, except in the case of brief quotations embodied in critical reviews and certain other noncommercial uses permitted by copyright law.

Published by My Kind of Story
Miami, Florida

Paperback ISBN: 979-8-218-88517-5
eBook ISBN: 979-8-218-81595-0
First Edition: October 2025
Revised Edition: December 2025

Cover design by David Arrate, using an image generated by Google Gemini.

This is a work of historical fiction. While it features real people, the dialogue, thoughts, and specific incidents portrayed are products of the author's imagination and are not to be construed as biographical fact.

For permissions, please use the contact form at:
mykindofstory.wordpress.com/contact/

"You know, your ma helped me realize somethin'. The way I figure it, if there's going to be hardship, regardless of what kind of man I decided on bein' ... well, I want to rest in peace knowin' I struggled for somethin' that was worth it to me. I suppose it's sort of like livin' up to be the kind of fella that you can admire."

— Alan Gates (portrayed by Henry Fonda), in *Pick Up the Gun, My Son*

Orson Welles was developing his adaptation of Othello and taking on additional acting work to fund the project when he was approached by Tyrone Power with a script and an opportunity to direct.

Pick Up the Gun, My Son *was a Western adapted from a novella by its author, who credited Power for sparking its creation. It was originally slated to be made with Edmund Goulding, who had directed Power in two films following the actor's return from military service during World War II:* The Razor's Edge *(1946) and* Nightmare Alley *(1947). But the box office failure of the latter—another personal project for Power—prevented him from obtaining financial support from producer Darryl F. Zanuck, then head of 20th Century Fox, where Power remained under contract.*

Popular for his swashbuckler and romantic leading roles, Power was growing frustrated with his career. His handsome looks had proved a marketable asset for Fox, and the studio, in fear of losing his image, had shown reluctance at granting its star's longing for more complex and challenging roles. As a result, Power would vent his frustration, wishing he could release himself from the limitations of beauty—for something more meaningful.

Author and screenwriter Tracy Little was born in the spring of 1923. The younger of two children in a poor white Appalachian family from Tennessee, she fell in love with movies after seeing Sergeant York *(1941), starring Gary Cooper, at the age of eighteen. Her obsession with the medium ignited her desire to write, and nearly three years later she published her first short story—a rural thriller dedicated to Cooper and to director Howard Hawks.*

Little's approach to "fishing for ideas," as she called it, was to imagine pairing an actor with an actress—or a film director—and to create an ideal scenario that would bring characters to life in her mind. This method provided the raw material for a story, but the process was also an act of self-revelation. It often served to reveal and heal old wounds. At the same time, it allowed Little to acknowledge her own passions and abilities.

Like many moviegoers, Little admired matinee idol Tyrone Power. Upon reading of his professional discontent, she was prompted to write what would become her most intimate tale to date. With the help of her editor, Power was contacted through his agent and given an advance copy of the story, soon to appear in a pulp magazine. Grateful, the actor purchased the rights and, after a brief correspondence, hired Little to adapt it for the screen.

Welles and Power spent several months trying to raise the capital needed to fund the production. Welles sought investors in Europe while Power persisted with the major studios back home. By this time, Fox had permitted Power to seek roles elsewhere, provided he fulfilled his studio commitments between these external projects.

One obstacle was the story's call for Power's face to be made up—rendering him nearly unrecognizable and devoid of glamour—which in turn required another major star to help sell the unusual "psychological" Western. Eventually, the project attracted the attention of actor James Stewart and director Anthony Mann. Mann persuaded Welles and Power that he could secure financial backing if granted the directorial reins, and the project finally began to move forward. Welles quickly rewrote the villain's role for himself, and Stewart officially joined the cast.

However, shortly before filming was scheduled to begin, Mann dropped out due to creative differences with both Welles and Power—and Stewart left with him. "Power's baby," as it had come to be known, now risked losing its financiers.

But Zanuck proved sympathetic to Power's plight. He intervened by helping attract director Fritz Lang, while Power sought out his former co-star Henry Fonda and persuaded him to take over the role that had belonged to Stewart. Performing on Broadway at the time, Fonda reluctantly agreed, but only under certain terms and working hours.

Fonda had twice sworn never to work with Lang again —first after You Only Live Once *(1937), and again after* The Return of Frank James *(1940). Lang's demanding, authoritarian style, honed in Europe, was notoriously difficult for some Hollywood actors, including Spencer Tracy. Still, Power, having just worked with Lang on* American Guerrilla in the Philippines *(1950), was prepared for the challenge. With the support of both Power and Welles, Fonda's third and final outing with Lang proved to be a professional and ultimately rewarding collaboration. This last successful partnership brought the film's fraught production to a close, and* Pick Up the Gun, My Son *was released in the autumn of 1951.*

The resulting film bore the unmistakable aesthetic of its director: a deliberate clash between the innocent, vibrant palette of a children's storybook and a dark, noirish mood. A key component of this was a visual style that benefited greatly from Lang's early training as a painter in his native Austria and his mastery of the mood and tension found in German Expressionism and film noir.

Pick Up the Gun, My Son tells the story of two starkly different lives that intertwine not on a familiar desert plain, but in the dense forests of a remote northwestern town. The first belongs to twelve-year-old Bobby Gates, a kind, gentle, and compassionate innocent.

The film opens beneath a mountain creek, the camera directed toward the surface, moving slowly with the current. Before it halts beneath a pair of small feet, a quote from the ninth-century Sufi mystic Mansur al-Hallaj appears: *"I saw my Lord with the eye of the heart. I asked, 'Who art Thou?' He answered, 'Thou.'"*

We first see Bobby in a close-up through the eyes of a young girl. They sit beside each other on the bank of the creek, cooling their bare feet in the water. We see her through his eyes, as she awaits his kiss, which he delicately bestows in a follow-up close two-shot. As we will come to find out, he is a boy defined by the legacy of his parents: his father, a reformed outlaw turned family man, has just returned from a three-month cattle drive; his mother, a saintly woman who soothed her husband's wilder instincts, has instilled in her son the desire to find and live up to his potential.

One night, after learning of his father's past as a rustler, Bobby asks his mother what she saw in the man she married.

"The same thing he wanted to be," she replies. "A good,

strong man."

Inspired by his mother's unorthodox faith, Bobby aspires to be more like Christ, whom she greatly admires—though, in his young eyes, she interprets the Bible metaphorically. Heeding her advice to learn from the past, he listens closely to the stories of his elders. Through tales of heroes and outlaws, he begins to understand the world's dual nature —and the capacity for good and evil in everyone. This awareness becomes the seed of his spiritual quest. He quickly turns it into a game, asking his playmates to "test" his character and, in turn, to reflect on their own.

SCENE: **ROLE PLAYING**

A neighboring tomboy and bully, Shannon Henry, is supposed to be watching her little sister while her father works the plow on their farm. Instead, her attention is fixed on Bobby Gates. We see her resentment as she watches the other children—particularly the smaller boys and girls—drawn to him. This animosity, however, masks a secret crush.

Bobby has the children engaged in a new kind of role-playing, a clear departure from their usual games of Cowboys and Indians. Shannon sees the strangeness of this new game as an opportunity to get him in trouble. Mocking him from a distance, she plants her hands on her hips and calls out:

Shannon Henry: Bobby Gates, if you're God, then I'm the Devil!

Bobby pauses from his chores. He regards her not with anger, but with the patient smile of someone recognizing a familiar pattern.

Bobby: All right. It's no fun being one if there's not the other. ... We can take turns!

Shannon's challenge is instantly deflated, and she sighs in frustration.

The film's other protagonist—the part written for Tyrone Power—is a bounty hunter in his mid-thirties. He masks his face with a dark blue bandana pulled up over his nose, focusing all attention on his intense, watchful eyes. A deep, jagged scar runs down his forehead and across his right eyebrow, brutally marring the actor's familiar features. We learn his story in fragments: that the scarred man we see now was once a handsome child, and that his disfigurement is the result of a single, brutal act of cruelty from his youth.

On a stormy night, a lone figure waits in ambush—mounted on his horse atop a hill, silhouetted beside a burnt-out tree. Two riders approach on the trail below; one has a price on his head. A flash of lightning reveals the bounty hunter's position, and a chase erupts. He drops the second man with a shot to the back, while the fugitive, blinded by the rain, rides frantically off a cliff.

Horse and rider crash through the tree branches below. The animal dies on impact, pinning the helpless man beneath its weight. Through the storm, he watches his pursuer navigate the slippery, rocky slope, drawing a gun to finish the job.

Giancarlo Polo, the villain played by Orson Welles, was nine years old when his family arrived in the Midwest, part of the surge of European immigrants during the American

Civil War. Now in his early forties, he is a big, burly man with a thick mustache and prematurely graying hair. He leads a gang of guns-for-hire in the service of the territory's two most powerful cattle barons. They call him "Charlie" Polo.

When Polo's gang rides into town, their reputation precedes them, spreading in hushed whispers. Their leader, they say, is "as smooth as the Devil." Their presence is immediately unsettling, rousing the tempers of townspeople, ranchers, and farmers alike. Yet neither Polo nor his men reveal whether they act for their employers' interests or their own.

From the moonlit image of the bounty hunter's gun, the scene cuts to day for a close-up of another man's hand firing a round into the air. The camera swoops in on the antagonist as he lets out a great, booming laugh. He watches the town's hired prostitutes run into the woods to begin a chase—sport for him and his gang. This "Picnic Sequence," as Welles called it, was one of his own revisions, reportedly inspired by Charles Chaplin's dance with the wood nymphs in the 1919 silent film *Sunnyside.*

One of the women, a Norwegian immigrant, runs playfully beside another prostitute before taking cover beneath a thick brush. From her hiding spot, she sees Bobby and his father steering a team and wagon toward town. She watches them, curious, until one of Polo's men suddenly leaps upon her from behind. A comical shriek escapes her lips.

The father and son arrive in town for supplies—a rare chance for quality time together—unaware that Polo and his scoundrels have since taken it over.

Inside the general store, the scene is quiet. Alan Gates, the man played by Henry Fonda, gently examines a pair of women's shoes. We sense that his thoughts are on his wife, Hannah—the woman who, for him, represents everything good in the world and in himself.

The film reveals Hannah's past later, in a conversation between Bobby and a reformed Shannon Henry. We learn that Hannah was in her mid-teens when the man who would become her husband—a former Confederate soldier turned outlaw—rescued her. Her family, pilgrims banished from their colony for unorthodox beliefs, had been murdered by "some savage Indian tribe." The intimate faith of her parents lives on in the way Hannah's own family worships.

Karen Lee Venk, the film's leading actress, was discovered by Lang years earlier during his travels across the United States. It was Lang who encouraged her parents to send her to modeling school, a path that led her to Hollywood. Pick Up the Gun, My Son *would be her only screen appearance. During filming, she fell in love with a set designer, and the couple soon married. As fate would have it, they became neighbors with Little's family, and Karen Lee and the author would remain lifelong friends.*

A short time later, inside a saloon called The Lazy Yank, Polo's men are spurring on the excitement. At a private table upstairs, Polo himself plays "a friendly game of cards" with the town's bank owner and mayor. The mayor's puppet marshal stands guard nearby—a silent testament to the true power in the room.

Beside Polo sits his closest confidant, Tom Locke, a

grizzled and world-weary older man and former cookie. Locke has no family, only the treacherous company he rides with. He feels time running out. The lifelong routine of siding with untrustworthy men is eating away at what remains of his soul.

A farmer suddenly approaches their table and confronts Polo, accusing him of stealing his land. Polo only laughs. As the marshal nervously takes the man's arm to escort him out, Polo teases, "You take it from the Indian, I take it from you."

Just then, the saloon doors swing open. Polo's most volatile and infamous gunman arrives, flanked by his two cronies, Levi and Buster. Played by the great Dan Duryea, the wiry gunslinger's name is Carson, though he's earned a more notorious moniker: *"Crazy."*

SCENE: **CRAZY'S IN TOWN**

An upset saloon girl vents her outrage. A steady customer—a cowboy who'd been saving his earnings to take her away—has headed off to Alaska, seeking fortune without her. The bar patrons are pouring her drinks, waiting to take advantage of her later. "Crazy" Carson walks over, curiously amused.

Saloon Girl: I wasted two years of my life waiting on that no-good, lying cowpoke!

"Crazy" Carson: You planning on wasting another two crying about it?

While the other men have failed to humor her, Carson is the first to actually draw a smile from her face.

Saloon Girl: I like the way you think, handsome.

She throws her arms around his neck.

Saloon Girl: I bet you've got a couple of sweethearts tucked away somewhere.

"Crazy" Carson: At least two in every town.

Carson laughs into her face and she laughs back. He helps himself to one of her drinks.

Saloon Girl: So how many you got stashed here in Mulgachaw?

"Crazy" Carson: This town? Honey, I just rode in.

The bounty hunter—the man played by Power—reemerges outside the Reynolds home, neighbors of the Gates family. Inside, Shelley Reynolds is alone in the kitchen preparing supper. She cries out in fright when she sees the masked face peering through her open window. In a calm voice, the bounty hunter asks for directions to the nearest town.

He makes a slow, teasing suggestion that any thief could enter her home, testing her mettle. When he discovers she is armed with only a broomstick, he offers her the dead, wanted man's gun for protection. As she takes it, she nervously wonders aloud how she'll explain the new weapon to her suspicious and jealous husband.

The bounty hunter turns to go.

"I reckon that's your business, ma'am."

During dinner, the conversation between Alan and Hannah Gates is tense, filled with troubling stories gathered from neighbors and weary travelers about the new men in town. For now, they agree to wait, hoping Polo's gang is simply passing through. Alan weighs the potential for violence, but Hannah believes a lesson in humility would be more effective.

In a moment that captures her unorthodox and fiery spirit, she declares that such men need to be run out of town, stripped naked, mounted on their horses, and sent "back into the wilderness."

In the tradition of Hannah's upbringing, the family joins hands to say grace in silence. For her, worship is a private act, treated with an intimacy that some of the other families frown upon. They insist she and her son should join them for public church services, but Hannah holds fast to her faith.

The scene cuts to the raucous interior of The Lazy Yank saloon. The place is packed. On stage, surrounded by saloon girls, Charlie Polo gives a booming performance of "Questa o quella" from Verdi's *Rigoletto.* (Welles's voice is clearly dubbed, though by an accredited tenor.) He pours beer down a woman's throat while waving a cluster of flowers —a grand mockery of his youthful ambition to become an opera singer.

Into this chaos walks the bounty hunter. He's been directed here to find Marshal Howell and collect his reward.

Throughout her pulp stories, Little often explored a difficult and recurring question: why suffering seems necessary for the forging of the human spirit. *This theme is confronted most directly in her penultimate work, a thriller titled "My Son*

Is Missing."

It tells the tale of a divorced father who, dissatisfied with his city life and job, convinces himself that his ex-wife has kidnapped their son. Frustrated by a lack of progress in the case and the low morale within a corrupt police department, he finally lashes out when provoked by a cruel senior officer.

"Yeah, I've got a problem!" he tells him. "And thank God I found out what it was. I've finally understood that a man's gonna have to struggle, no matter what road he takes. But when he settles down with fear and idleness, he lets go of his dreams. That's why most of us end up struggling for something that doesn't mean anything to him. It bends us and makes us crooked. You know the saying that 'Misery loves company,' Bud? There's your root of all evil."

The scene from "My Son Is Missing" ends on an upbeat note. The older detective follows his young colleague outside, offers him a cigarette, and—in a wry, personal touch from the author—tries to humor him by confessing he'd always wanted to be a cowboy instead of a cop.

Little enjoyed walking out of a movie or away from a story feeling "strong, inspired, and charged," as she would say. While she valued relating to the material, she also cherished laughing and smiling along with the characters.

"My wife is plainspoken and full of vigor," her husband once wrote to a friend. "It's a wonder my head hasn't split open from all the laughing she gets out of me."

Those who knew her felt that the character of Bobby Gates was the purest reflection of this joyful spirit. Bobby's enthusiastic, butterfly-net approach to collecting wisdom makes him one of the most sympathetic personalities in the story. Wielding a charisma inherited from his mother, he is particularly effective with the younger children. He is also regarded with affection by the grandfatherly general store owner, Old John, who delights in the boy's attentive and cheerful demeanor—a stark contrast to his own son, a "good-for-nothing, pigheaded vermin" named Sherman.

The young, native Kentuckian actor who played Bobby Gates brought a natural charm and wit essential to the role. He would go on to appear in only one other film: the lean, action-packed 1952 Scott–Brown production, When You Hear the Drums.

Based on an original screenplay by Little, it starred Randolph Scott as an Indian brave who shares a silent, mutual admiration with a fearless frontierswoman as they unknowingly pursue the same missing person. The film became briefly popular for influencing the sale of toy bows and arrows, as well as shoe polish and lipstick—the last two items used by children to imitate the opening close-up of Scott having war paint applied to his face.

"I think it's easier to just write about villains, wimps, and weasels," Little once said. "But when it comes to developin' genuine heroes... once I get 'em right, I find it's the most rewardin' part of storytellin'."

For Little, a hero who was good simply for the sake of being good was the dullest character imaginable. She believed that true character, heroic or villainous, was forged in the crucible of suffering. Like her villains, her heroes needed a powerful motivation.

"The greater the motive," she said, "the better the story."

The newly arrived Carson has already killed a man. We learn through eyewitness accounts that his victim was the "stubborn sodbuster" who confronted Polo earlier and failed to leave peaceably.

The bounty hunter descends the saloon staircase, having just spoken with a drunken deputy. He pauses on the last step as he hears Polo yell out, *"Ciao, bambino!"* Across the room, Polo and Carson flank a tall, robust redhead, linking arms with her. The trio then turns and merrily makes their way directly toward the bounty hunter.

Power's character flattens himself against the wall at the foot of the stairs. The camera takes his point of view as the towering figure of Polo brushes past him and heads up the steps toward the private rooms above.

He forgets his search for the marshal. He watches Polo disappear up the stairs, a flicker of uncertain recognition in his eyes. *Is this a figure from his past?*

The question triggers a fractured, violent memory.

A flashback: a sun-dappled creek. A handsome boy of about twelve or thirteen admires his reflection in the water while fishing. The peaceful image is shattered by the sudden appearance of four older teens. One of them, who resembles a young Charlie Polo, sneers that the boy "looks like a girl." The others drag him, struggling, into the reeds.

The memory is fleeting, but the torment it resurrects will now haunt him for the rest of the film.

It is here that we learn the bounty hunter answers to the name Beau Jagger—a man given not only a face, but a past that refuses to let him rest.

Up to this point, Power's performance has relied solely on his eyes, posture, and voice. But that changes when he finally locates Marshal Howell. After learning of Polo's meeting with the mayor and bank owner, Jagger removes his bandana, revealing a ghastly, terribly scarred face and a thick mustache. From the frightened marshal, he learns the truth: Charlie Polo is set to seize a great deal of wealth, which he intends to use to consolidate power in this part of the country—with the town's leaders already in his pocket.

The following morning, just before sunup, Jagger follows Polo and his men as they ride toward the Holston Cattle Ranch to begin their takeover.

Inside the ranch parlor, Polo shaves, his face lathered in the mirror. Reflected in the glass, we see Tom Locke standing outside, looking in through the window. Locke is Holston's inside man, and we sense his shame; he failed to warn the cattleman of Polo's betrayal. The plan had come together too quickly, literally overnight, leaving him no chance to reach Holston first.

While veteran actor Henry Hull served as Little's model for the store owner, Old John, she wrote the part of cattle baron Jesse Holston specifically for Walter Huston. Huston was contacted for the role, but he unfortunately passed away shortly after completing another Western—Anthony Mann's The Furies *(1950).*

SCENE: **THE TROUBLE WITH CHARLIE**

Cattle baron Jesse Holston looks across his own parlor, now overrun with killers, and sees everything he's built about to be stolen. His foreman, "Charlie" Polo, stands facing him defiantly, one boot pinning down Holston's spoiled son.

Polo contemptuously empties a wooden shaving bowl of its dirty water onto the young man's head, then drops the bowl to the floor. He reaches back to the fireplace mantle, grabs a hand towel, and dries himself with a confident smile.

Jessie Holston: You've got some pretty highfalutin 'ideas in that head of yours. It must be numb being so dumb with greed. Pretty soon you'll be wanting more. And more, and more!

Charlie Polo *(chuckling)*: Maybe I get that from you, Holly.

Two of Polo's men, Buster and Shipp, move to block the door, cutting off any chance of escape. Holston glances over, the realization dawning: they mean to kill him. He slowly places his hands behind his back, carefully reaching for a pocket pistol tucked into his waistband.

Jessie Holston: I figure that maybe you did. You know what your trouble is, Charlie? You've got the guts, but you don't know how to use 'em.

He pauses, fingers finding the gun.

Jessie Holston: Yeah, sure, you might be the last mistake I ever make. But sooner or later, it's gonna be your hide those vultures will be turning their guns on.

Buster sees Holston's hand move and draws his sidearm.

Buster: Watch it! The old man's got a gun!

Charlie Polo: Let him!

Polo's sudden shout makes Holston flinch. His pistol gets stuck in his waistband as he fumbles to draw. In a fluid motion, Polo draws his gun and fires—square in the chest.

Holston's eyes widen, his jaw drops. His body sways. Polo fires again. The second bullet knocks the old man off his feet.

Locke looks from the fallen body of his former employer to the cold, heartless eyes of his new boss. Polo, having already won over the majority of Holston's cowhands, gives his final order:

"Have some fun. Then make the fire."

The film portrays Bobby's first love—the young girl from the opening scene—entirely without dialogue. Their relationship is never spoken of, but expressed through quiet closeness, shared looks, and smiles when they are among the other children.

One afternoon, two older boys find Bobby walking home alone. One of them is Sherman, the general store owner's son. They taunt and threaten him. When Sherman insults Hannah, parroting gossip he's heard from the church women, Bobby connects a hard right hook to his jaw. The other boy jumps in, and Sherman retaliates with a flurry of manic slaps. The editing of the scene creates a menacing atmosphere that feels far more brutal than the actual fight.

Finally, Sherman's mother arrives, pulling her son away by the ear. After belittling Bobby, she orders him home. There, alone with his mother, a discouraged Bobby confesses everything. Hannah now understands the source of the growing resentment toward her family. While their neighbors may call her son a blasphemer, she sees only his faith.

Reviving his will with her tenderness, she gestures toward his heart and tells him,

"You can't expect people with no faith in themselves to have any in you. Least of all, in Him."

Under a full moon, concealed within the hills, Jagger watches as Polo's men set a bungalow on Holston's ranch ablaze. As he crouches in the shadows, the camera moves in on his face, and the film's visual narrative gives way to a storm of sound.

We hear the scene in the style of a radio drama: a young boy's pleas, the sounds of a struggle, the tearing of clothing —all insinuating an unspeakable horror. As the soundscape builds, the image of the bounty hunter's face is brought to the foreground in three sharp cuts. The third fills the screen with the dark, pained pools of Power's eyes. The fourth pushes in on a single eye, and a new image is superimposed over it: a low-angle shot, as if looking up from the ground. In this new image, a heavyset teen turns to leave—the very same one from Jagger's earlier memory. He suddenly stops, looks down at his victim, and a cruel smile spreads across his face. Then, he taunts: *"Ciao, bambino."*

A great deal of Power's direction for this scene came from Little's original script and Lang's passion for meticulous detail. The choice to present the flashback audibly, while keeping the visual memory locked within the character, was a key element. Welles incorporated this subjective, point-of-view aesthetic into the shooting script before handing it to Lang, thereby realizing a stylization he had attempted years earlier in his unrealized adaptation of Joseph Conrad's Heart of Darkness *(1899). Little would later praise Welles for his contributions, claiming he added a level of intensity exactly where it was needed.*

The following morning, a shootout erupts between Jagger and Polo's men on the trail. The camera adopts Jagger's perspective as he hangs sideways from his saddle, firing in the foreground. He mortally wounds Buster but is ultimately caught, bound, and dragged back to town for an extended period of retribution.

There, a dying Buster is about to execute their prisoner when Marshal Howell intervenes. In a final act of cold-blooded violence, Buster murders the lawman instead. Hearing the gunshot and ensuing chaos, Tom Locke grimly remarks that he can hear "Mr. Holston laughing from the grave." With the marshal's murder, Polo's gang has gone too far. The townspeople begin calling for action.

The pistol Jagger gave to Mrs. Reynolds soon finds its way into Hannah's hands. Her friend Shelley—now armed with a rifle provided by her husband—is desperate to rid herself of the incriminating handgun.

Returning home alone after visiting her friend, Hannah is attacked by Levi and Carson, both drunk and mourning their fallen companion, Buster. She's forced to use the pistol in self-defense—Levi takes a bullet in the face—but in the struggle, Carson shoots and kills her.

Drawn by the gunfire, Alan Gates is the first to arrive. He finds Hannah lifeless on the floor just as Carson flees. He has only a moment to register the horror before a cold rage takes over. He trails Carson into the darkness. The gunman is quick on the draw, but Alan, from his outlaw days, was faster—and a better marksman.

Moments later, Bobby returns home to find the house eerily still. He discovers his mother lying on the wooden floor, her bare back to the camera. In the film's most heartbreaking moment, the boy gently covers her and weeps, until gunfire from outside forces him to act.

SCENE: **"PICK UP THE GUN"**

Alan Gates has tracked down and killed Carson, the man who murdered his wife. Wounded in the arm and leg, he collapses to his knees beside the body.

He looks around frantically, his eyes landing on the dead man's revolver just a few feet away. He tosses his own empty revolver aside in frustration just as his son, Bobby, arrives and takes in the terrible scene.

Alan Gates *(through gritted teeth)***:** Bobby… pick up the gun. Pick it up, son.

Bobby stares, his face a mask of horror and grief. When he finally speaks, his voice cracks:

Bobby: No, pa! Don't you see him? *(He gestures at Carson's body.)* You aimin' on doin' more killin'?!

He breaks down, sobbing.

Bobby: If it's too late for you... then take me, too... Ma's gone anyway...

The fury drains from Alan's face, replaced by the crushing weight of his son's words. He shakes his head, not in disagreement but in pained acceptance. He reaches for his boy, pulling him into a tight embrace.

Alan Gates *(voice thick with emotion)*: Help me up, son. Just… help me up.

Having been tortured and left tied up for further abuse, Jagger drifts in and out of consciousness. The physical pain gives rise to something deeper—a searing memory that will not stay buried.

A flashback. We see the handsome young Jagger from behind, weeping uncontrollably. In his mind, the mocking laughter of his attackers echoes, circling him like ghosts. In a moment of pure anguish, he brings a sharp object to his own face.

Out of this haze of memory and pain, Tom Locke appears. He uses an ivory-handled hunting knife—a gift from his former employer—to cut Jagger loose. His expression is grim, carved with years of regret. He knows death is close and is driven by one final need: to balance the ledger of his life by avenging the murders of the Holston family. He offers the knife to Jagger and asks for his help.

But before Locke can arm him, three of Polo's men burst onto the scene. The ensuing shootout is brief and furious, leaving Locke and the three gunmen dead. Wounded in the leg, Jagger manages to flee, tucking a pistol into his waistband and clenching Locke's knife between his teeth. He is not only bent on vengeance now, but on *recognition*—to make Polo remember him, to confirm that he is indeed the boy from his past.

Overwhelmed by grief, Alan Gates succumbs to a restless sleep, his final moments haunted by the memory of his son's tearful plea and their desperate embrace.

As his father lies still, Bobby makes a decision. He takes the dead, wanted man's gun, saddles a horse, and rides out into the night—intent on killing the one responsible for bringing the man who took his mother: Charlie Polo.

SCENE: **"WHY?"**

Bobby encounters his neighbors, Mark and Shelley Reynolds, on the trail into town as they retrieve their livestock. Mark, a bitter and cynical farmer, accuses Bobby of being "kinfolk to the Devil" before spitting on the ground and returning to his work.

But Shelley, who longs for a better life than the misery that has crippled her husband, calls out for Bobby to wait. In the darkness, she cannot see the despair on his face or know that his mother is dead.

Miss Shelley: I think your mother is a wonderful woman. She came by this afternoon, and we talked about you and the other children. *(Shelley smiles, as she struggles with her emotions.)* I think it's brave of you—pretending to understand why God does what He does. *(She lets out a short, nervous laugh.)* I wish I could play too. If just to figure out if... if this is all I have to give.

Bobby is quiet for a moment. He recognizes her pain—her feeling of purposelessness. A faint, knowing smile touches his lips as his eyes glisten with gratitude for his mother's wisdom.

Bobby: Why do you want children, Miss Shelley?

His faith restored, Bobby reclaims the reins of his emotions and carries on with a new aim. A wide shot shows the surrounding wooded bottomland as a new image is superimposed high above him: the smiling, angelic spirit of his mother, Hannah. As Bobby's horse races below, her spirit soars as a silent guardian on his journey toward town.

Rain clouds have come and gone, turning the unpaved streets to mud. Vowing to avenge their slain, Polo and his men are turning the town upside down. Unseen, Jagger crawls through the soft, wet earth beneath the boardwalks, taking them down one by one with Locke's knife.

Outside a gambling den called the Annie Chuck Club, Bobby finds Polo. Charlie Polo storms through the swinging batwing doors and steps into the street, demanding blood for blood. Bobby freezes, having never met the man face to face.

Brandishing two pistols, Polo sneers, "God has forgotten you, boy."

Bobby finds his voice, his reply immediate: "It's you who's been doin' the forgettin', sir!"

Just then, Jagger rises from the mud behind him and plunges the knife between his shoulder blades. Polo cries out, squeezing off a wild shot as he falls. The bullet grazes Bobby's head.

Stunned, Bobby slumps in the saddle. His horse, spooked by the gunshot, bolts. As Bobby falls, his foot gets caught in the stirrup, and he is dragged helplessly through the mud.

An angry mob of townspeople swarms the fallen bodies of Polo and Jagger. A man yells, "Let's send 'em packin'!" The low camera angle captures the chaos: the mob moving one way, the terrified horse dragging the unconscious boy in the other.

The panicked animal finally slows, coming to a stop

near a creek bed. The camera cuts to a close-up of Bobby's limp form. A bright, glowing woman's hand, superimposed, reaches into the frame from above and gently caresses his face.

Bobby slowly comes to. Another rider is there, having calmed his horse. It's Jagger, freeing the boy's foot from the stirrup.

"Am I dead, sir?" Bobby asks.

"No, boy," Jagger responds.

The camera moves in tight on Bobby's eyes. Reflected in them, we see a scarless, redeemed Beau Jagger. A quiet understanding passes between them.

"Looks like there's still life in you," Jagger says, his voice quiet. "And in me."

In addition to his rewrites, Welles also storyboarded key sequences for the film. It's believed they influenced some of Lang's decisions, particularly with the more fantastic images —the very same visual stylization that Anthony Mann had clashed with.

Having invested his own money in the production, Power refused Mann's wishes to minimize the dialogue and remove Hannah's spirit from the film's ending. Welles stood by Power, agreeing that these elements were essential to the story's unique tone and texture. As for Lang, whose early career was built on both art films and popular entertainment, he relished the opportunity to blend the two.

Bobby's final ride into town inspired an original oil painting used for the French theatrical poster, which was considered one of the most striking of its day. It depicted the boy racing through the woods while an angelic Hannah hovered overhead.

In France, the film was released under the title Les Pauvres Diables *(The Poor Devils).*

Reviewers of the day noted the film's exploration of themes beyond revenge. One contributor to the newly created Cahiers du Cinéma *wrote that it focused on "mending the wounded spirit, set out on a frontier of the Old American West." Of course, these critics couldn't have known that the author's true motivation was to explore the spirit of a woman—her own—and that the story itself had become her means of making sense of a private trauma.*

Despite the usual challenges of a Fritz Lang set—his autocratic style and frustrating demand for precise details—his methods ultimately served the very vision that Power and Welles had championed from the start. Lang's demanding approach clearly paid off, as the cast, crew, and author were all deeply proud of the finished film. Little would later admit, however, her initial disappointment over James Stewart's early departure, confessing she had originally written the character of Alan Gates with him in mind.

"I liked Fonda," she told friends. "I thought he did good. He just ain't Jimmy Stewart, is all."

Legend has it that when Little met Stewart shortly after the film's premiere, she walked right up and gave him a light punch on the arm. A surprised Stewart found out who she was and offered his other arm for a second go. Before Little could accept, Stewart's wife took the swing herself—promptly followed by another jab from Ms. Little.

According to Little's children, the nickname their father used for their mother was coined that day. As Stewart was leaving, he turned and yelled out, "So long, Little Wonder!"

Little would return to the Western genre two more times. Her first project after Pick Up the Gun, My Son *was the aforementioned* When You Hear the Drums, *which she dedicated to her husband. After that film's release, she stepped away from writing for over a decade to focus on raising her children.*

Her third and last Western was a contemporary tale set in America's most famous city. Titled Git Along, Little Dog, *the children's adventure book was published shortly after her eldest son was drafted into the Army. The story follows another police detective's kidnapped boy in late-1960s New York. The young hero, nicknamed "Little Dog" Webb, dresses in a cowboy costume armed with a pair of noisy cap guns and finds himself in the midst of the counterculture movement—a land swarming with long-haired, "savage Indians." Teaming up with a homeless black youth nicknamed "Buckshot" Lewis, who plays Sancho Panza to his Don Quixote, "Little Dog" not only finds his way home but also saves a bus of GIs from being sabotaged.*

Little dedicated the book to her family, with special thanks to Norman Rockwell, whose illustrations influenced and lent shape to the story's imagery. Despite her prolific career in crime fiction, her children always loved her Westerns best. She, on the other hand, was said to have been proud of them all.

In light of the professional satisfaction she attained, examining Little's early history allows one to truly understand her accomplishments.

A frank look at Tracy's life reveals that she was both a runaway and a victim of molestation. Her daughter, Hannah, said that her mother struggled to articulate herself when she was younger. "But whenever someone corrected her," Hannah would say, "she was always quick to thank them. Mom had a genuinely sweet disposition. Whenever she'd say 'thank you' in her East Tennessee accent and smile—my brothers and I thought she was the most beautiful woman in the whole world."

Her quiet strength was what Rose Gast saw when she and Tracy worked together in a munitions factory during the war. It was there that Tracy's trust in others began its slow restoration. Knowing her son, Jeffrey, had a distaste for prissy girls, Mrs. Gast arranged an introduction.

Jeffrey was optimistic and bookish, studying to become an archaeologist. While Tracy loved pulp stories, he preferred history and mythology. This shared passion for storytelling drew them together, and they would talk for hours on end. It was Jeffrey who introduced her to the works of Mansur al-Hallaj. At the time, the poet's life was chronicled in a dense 1922 French study by Louis Massignon, making the quote virtually unknown to an English-speaking audience. Tracy would be the one to introduce it to the moviegoing public in the film's opening.

As their son, Jeffrey Jr., tells it, their real courtship began with a story. "Mom was on her way to visit our grandmother to share a movie idea she had, which wound up becoming her first short story, "Run, Mountain Man." Grandma arranged it so Dad would be there... She said our father was the one who taught her self-worth and encouraged her to cultivate the worlds she was putting on paper."

Determined to impress the knowledgeable young Gast, Tracy poured her energy into her stories, but soon found she was writing more to satisfy her own growing ambitions. She was, as she put it, stretching out her inner canvas.

When the Second World War ended, Jeffrey was spared from being shipped overseas and returned home. Arriving at the bus depot, he and Tracy were so excited that they embraced for the first time, and Tracy kissed his cheek. Their younger son commented, "Mom's face started glowing, while Dad's got red. Not long after the magazine publication of Pick Up the Gun*, the stork flew by to drop off Theo."*

Upon returning from his military service in Vietnam, Theo Gast dedicated himself to education and used the GI Bill to pursue a college degree. Having never finished grade school, Tracy was especially happy and exclaimed what she often said: that her children were her life's finest achievement.

While Theo was still in college, his mother expressed an interest in writing a second book for young readers—a creation myth. She had become fascinated with mythology ever since meeting her husband, and had pondered over inventing one throughout their life together. Though the story never came to fruition, she had verbally shared its core idea with Theo, and he would carry and share that idea throughout his career. Upon becoming an elementary schoolteacher specializing in English and literature, he decided to use the classroom to continue his mother's legacy based on her unfinished project.

Every school year, until the day he retired, Theo would assign his students the same single question, asking them to write a sentence, an essay, or a story in response; requiring only that it be turned in before the end of the year. The question would be waiting for them on the chalkboard on the first day of school, and it would remain there even after every student submitted their response.

The question was: "What would you want the meaning of life to be?"

"There were so many beautiful stories and ideas they shared," Theo said in an interview. "I kept picturing my mom standing at the front of the class and smiling.

There was one occasion, while I was explaining how they were allowed to express their answers, when a timid boy nervously blurted out a single word, phrasing it as a question: 'Completion?', he said. I think she would have loved that."

In 1974, Tracy Little oversaw the release of a single-volume anthology collecting her entire canon of short fiction. On the dedication page, she wrote: "For all who desire to live, to pursue, and experience the power of creation."

Tracy Little passed away in 1976, as did director Fritz Lang two months later. Little was fifty-three years old; Lang was eighty-five.

The closing caption to Pick Up the Gun, My Son *reads:*

"Neither peace nor harmony can flourish upon the Earth unless the root is nourished within thee. He that listens to the voice of the heart, which yearns to realize its ultimate potential, shall find his path. And this journey shall prepare him for the greatest collaboration to come. Namely, the apex of man."

AFTERWORD

The idea for this story is over twenty years old, and it came from a simple misunderstanding. While listening to an account of two men I had met at a film screening, I was told secondhand that one of them had been gang-raped as a boy in Latin America. During another, overlapping conversation, I was somehow led to believe that the other man had been one of his attackers.

The imagined scenario—a victim and one of his teenage assailants later becoming friends—stayed with me for years, as did a vivid image that struck me that night, which would evolve into the flashback scene with a young Beau Jagger being dragged into the reeds. Even at the time, I recall thinking the setting for that imagined scene resembled a Western, as my mind had painted a simple countryside landscape.

A few years prior, in 2001, while attending a film festival in Austin, Texas, hosted by Quentin Tarantino, I was recommended one of the best outlets for rare movies: Mark Johnston's Shocking Videos. Upon returning home, I wasted no time in requesting a mail-order catalog. Johnston's knowledge of movies, combined with his unapologetic sense of humor and the way he sold his wares, set him apart from everyone else. Even his email newsletters would crack me up.

As a teenager, I repeatedly attempted to write stories in different literary styles. While I had some success with poetry, my longer narratives always lost focus because they lacked structure. So in 2005, I gave myself some rules and turned to Mark Johnston's catalog for inspiration. I started with a simple exercise: composing three "write-ups" for movies that never existed, pairing real actors and directors. This led to a Charles Bronson Euro-crime tale directed by Fernando Di Leo, a Klaus Kinski vampire film helmed by Lucio Fulci, and a Samuel Fuller biker flick starring Claudio Brook.

The first of these led to a project I began to outline as a novel, but after several drafts, I realized the idea needed more time to develop. It was then that the desire for a fourth write-up surfaced: the Western born from that imagined rape scene.

A second idea that contributed to the story's development came to me in a dream. I was riding a horse off a cliff during a rainstorm, and I was being shot at. I vividly recall crashing through the tree branches below as a masked man approached with his gun drawn, ready to kill me.

So in 2010, I dove into the genre, researching and watching Westerns from the '30s to the early '60s. In doing so, I quickly rediscovered the same love my grandfather had shared with me as a boy, with films like *Shane* (1953) and *The Outlaw* (1943).

My initial concept for this fourth write-up was a contemporary one: a mid-90s Western directed by Martin Scorsese and starring Tom Cruise. But as I began writing,

I realized the classic Hollywood era was a more suitable home for this story. And when I thought of another handsome, terrific actor from that period and read about his real-life frustration with being typecast, I was convinced: Tyrone Power was the bounty hunter.

With years 'worth of scenes and ideas pouring from my imagination, the first draft of *Pick Up the Gun, My Son* was written in a single night. This was followed by more than five months of historical research to expand the world and its characters. By the fall of 2010, I thought the story was finished, and it was released as a PDF on my blog in April of 2011. There it remained, unchanged, for many years.

In December of 2010, a funny scene between two actors who had never worked together popped into my head. I recognized right away that it was another Western, and its audacity and potential continue to obsess me to this day. But while many of the components were there, the story was missing its driving force.

The breakthrough came in the fall of 2024, with the introduction of a major new character and while reflecting on who I had written *Pick Up the Gun* for. With Tracy Little's story in mind, I understood my second Western needed its own muse—a new person to serve as its heart. That fresh dedication brought the motive I had been searching for, and the missing pieces finally fell into place.

In late August of 2025, I felt compelled to return to *Pick Up the Gun*—both for renewed stimulation and to prepare it for a proper release. It's been a very rewarding experience: weaving in additional images and ideas that have lingered in my mind, while reconnecting with this novelette that has been a part of my life for over two decades.

During this process, I mostly listened to Burning Sky's album *Blood of the Land*—the song "Abalone Heart," in particular, made me think of Bobby. Around the same time, I discovered "Return to Me" by October Project. The song hooked me instantly, as it perfectly matched the spiritual tone of Little's Western. Even now, its haunting mood and lyrics continue to drown out all other thoughts. Its themes feel like a perfect echo of Jagger and Bobby's tale: a loving spirit calling a lost soul back from the darkness, and redemption as a journey home to the self. "Return to Me" gave me the encouragement I needed, reassuring me that this story which had mattered so much to me was worth sharing.

Pick Up the Gun, My Son is dedicated to my mother, who gave me my love for books and a deep appreciation for history and biblical stories. She gave me a foundation of morals and human values, but always allowed me the freedom to discover my own faith.

Thank you for reading.

COMING SOON

Within the mother's womb, dreams were born.

Combining sounds, inspired by her muffled world,
with dances of light,
and changing warmth for cold and heat,
a universe was created,
followed by others.

Teeming with life,
they would endure and thrive
until all that was possible
was realized.

Revealed in the end
was the path to begin,
with the knowledge to answer:

Who am I?

Where am I?

What am I capable of?

If this story sounds familiar,
it's because it is yours.

—*Bandit Country*

ABOUT THE AUTHOR

Born and raised in Miami, Florida, David Arrate draws inspiration from a lifelong love of literature, history, film, music, and old-time radio. These passions shaped his debut Western novelette, *Pick Up the Gun, My Son.* He is now writing his second Western, a comic book mini-series.

For updates on this and future projects, you can connect with him at his blog, My Kind of Story:

mykindofstory.wordpress.com.

Made in the USA
Coppell, TX
19 January 2026